Bah! Humbug?

Lorna Balian

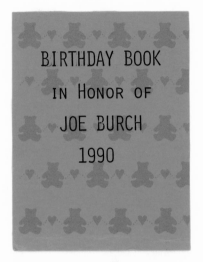

BIRTHDAY BOOK
IN HONOR OF
JOE BURCH
1990

BAH! HUMBUG?

Library of Congress Cataloging in Publication Data

BALIAN, LORNA
Bah! Humbug?
Summary: Two children set a trap for Santa Claus but
only one of them manages to see him.
(1. Santa Claus—Fiction. 2. Christmas stories)
I. Title.
PZ7.B1978Bah   (E)   76-50625
ISBN 0-687-37107-4

Previously published under ISBN 0–687-02345-9

MANUFACTURED BY THE PARTHENON PRESS AT
NASHVILLE, TENNESSEE, UNITED STATES OF AMERICA

For Arthur and Margie

Dear Santa Claus

    My brother Arthur says there is no
Santa Claus and I am wasting my time
writing to you but he is wrong lots of
times and I know you are really and truly
you.   I would like you to bring me
some ice skates and a new teddy bear
cause my old bear Herold has a worn
out belly. And anything else you think
a good little girl would like.

                Love
                Margie

            Santa Claus
             the North Pole

Arthur says that Santa Claus is a big fat humbug. Arthur says he can prove it and I have to help him and it's a secret and if I tell anybody he will put worms in my bed.

Arthur says he is collecting all the stuff we will need to carry out his big plan and we must hide everything until the time is right.

I hung up our stockings and put some cookies and milk
on the table cause it is Christmas Eve and I know Santa

Claus will come and he will be hungry when he gets here.
Arthur says it's all dum but Arthur is wrong lots of times.

Arthur says that after Mama and Daddy go to bed it will be time to put his plan into action.

Arthur says I better stay awake or he will put ice cubes in my pajamas.

Arthur says I must tiptoe

quiet as a mouse

and if I make any noise

he will flush Herold

down the toilet.

Arthur says he is making a grand trap to catch a big fat humbug Santa Claus. Arthur put a pail of cold water in the fireplace and a can of pennies by the door.

Arthur tied wind chimes to the Christmas tree and
spread balloons all over the floor. Arthur is tying
string around everything and hanging bells on it.

Arthur says the trap is ready and now we hafta wait.

Arthur says if I fall asleep he will put bubble gum in my hair.

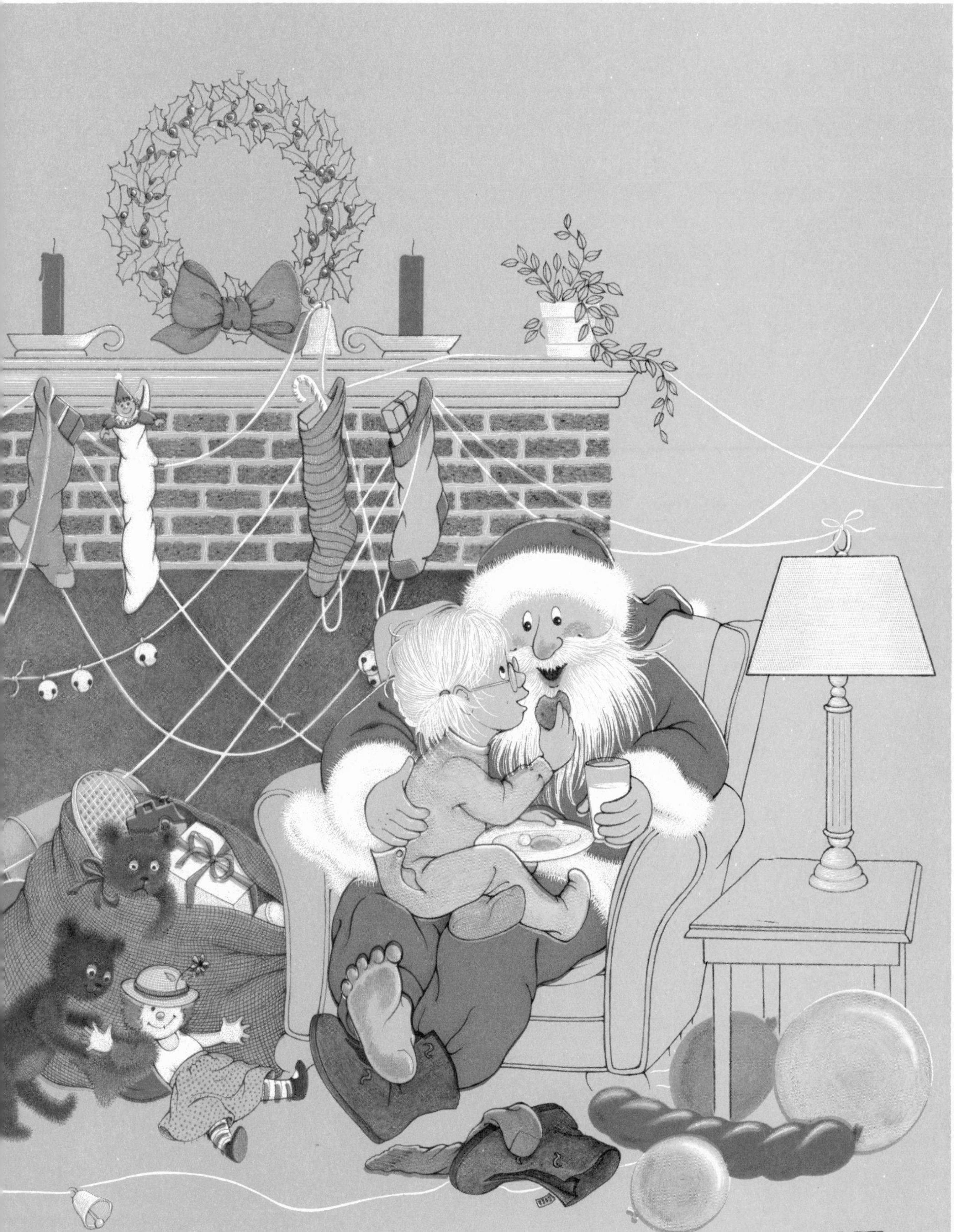

Arthur says maybe he was wrong about Santa Claus

but if I tell anybody he will mush peanut butter and jelly all over Herold's new fur coat.

Dear Santa Claus,

Thank you for the nice ice skates and for the new fuzzy coat for Herold and every thing. I knew you were really and truly you 'cause Arthur is wrong lots of Times.

Love

Margie